U.S. HOLIDAYS

Celebrate Martin Luther King Jr. Day

by Sally Lee

PEBBLE
a capstone imprint

First Facts are published by Pebble,
1710 Roe Crest Drive, North Mankato, Minnesota 56003
www.mycapstone.com

Library of Congress Cataloging-in-Publication Data
Library of Congress Cataloging-in-Publication data is available on the Library of Congress website.
ISBN 978-1-9771-0277-5 (library binding)
ISBN 978-1-9771-0533-2 (paperback)
ISBN 978-1-9771-0286-7 (eBook PDF)

Editorial Credits
Mandy Robbins, editor; Cynthia Della-Rovere, designer; Pam Mitsakos, media researcher; Tori Abraham, production specialist

Photo Credits
AP Photo: Paul Sakuma, 14-15; Getty Images: Bettmann, 6 (bottom right); iStockphoto: asiseeit, Cover, SolStock, 20-21, Steve Debenport, 18-19; Newscom: CNP/Arnie Sachs, 11, Everett Collection, 7, National Archives via CNP, 5, ZUMA Press/White House, 12-13; Shutterstock: Bokeh Blur Background, Design Element, Duda Vasilii, Design Element, EPG_EuroPhotoGraphics, 3 (bottom left), 17, sharpner, 1 (bottom); The Image Works: ©Syracuse Newspapers, 8-9

Quote Citation
Page 2, excerpted from "The Drum Major Instinct," a sermon by Rev. Martin Luther King, Jr., 1968.

Printed and bound in the United States of America.
PA49

King (right) speaks at a 1963 rally in Washington, D.C.

During King's life African-Americans had fewer rights than whites. Southern states had ***segregation*** laws. Blacks and whites could not use the same schools, bathrooms, or other public places. King led peaceful ***protests*** against these laws. The largest protest was the March on Washington.

Dr. King's Dream

In 1963 King helped lead the March on Washington. More than 250,000 people came to show their support for equal rights. At this march King gave his famous "I Have a Dream" speech. He dreamed of a country where everyone was treated equally.

There were even laws stating that whites and blacks had to drink from separate drinking fountains.

segregation—the practice of separating people according to groups, especially racial groups

protest—an action of a group of people who want something to be changed

The March on Washington convinced ***Congress*** to pass the Civil Rights Act in 1964. It outlawed segregation. President Lyndon B. Johnson signed the act into law. But King did not see all the results of his work. He was ***assassinated*** on April 4, 1968.

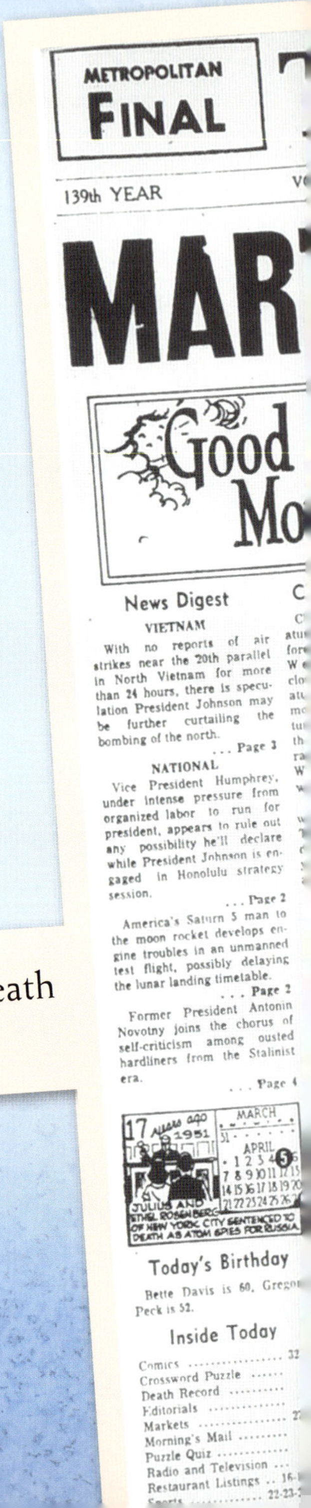

The news of King's death shocked the world.

Congress—the branch of a national government that makes laws

assassinate—to murder an important person

Cloudy, colder ... Chance of rain 30 per cent.

High today—48
Low tonight—30

[T]HE POST-STANDARD

10 CENTS
... Per Week Home Delivered

SYRACUSE, N. Y., FRIDAY, APRIL 5, 1968

... 203

[MART]IN LUTHER KING SLAIN

...ng

... Colder

...older temper... ...g winds are ...day by the ...reau. Partly ... cool temper... ...dicted for to... high tempera... be 48 degrees, ...30. Chances of ... 30 per cent. ...from the north... miles an hour. ...op temperature ...es, the low 46. ...perature was 56 ...grees above last ... and 15 degrees

... set at 6:35 p.m. ...e at 5:38 a.m. to... Vehicular lamps ...ted by 7:05 p.m.

...t for Today

...ther be right than ...t — Henry Clay, ...tatesman (177...

Shows Where Shot Hit

The Rev. Andrew Young, an aide to Dr. Martin Luther King, shows where Dr. King was hit by an assassin's bullet in Memphis, Tenn., last night. Young was pictured in the emergency room of St. Joseph's Hospital. (AP Wirephoto).

LBJ Says America Shocked

WASHINGTON (AP) — President Johnson spoke Thursday night of an "America shocked and saddened" by the assassination of Dr. Martin Luther King as he condemned violence, lawlessness and divisiveness.

In a brief, solemn message to the nation, Johnson disclosed that because of the slaying at Memphis he had canceled plans for a political appearance Thursday night and postponed until Friday his scheduled midnight departure for Hawaii and a Vietnam strategy conference.

The President appeared in the doorway of the White House offices, stern-faced and spoke on all television and radio networks.

"I ask every American citizen," he said, "to reject the blind violence that has struck down Dr. King, who lived by nonviolence."

The President urged prayers for peace and understanding in the land and said:

"We can achieve nothing by lawlessness and divisiveness among the American people."

He said he hopes all Americans would search their hearts.

At that point he said he was cancelling all plans for the evening and postponing until Friday his planned take-off for Hawaii and conferences there on problems of war and peace in Vietnam.

He was to have attended a Democratic fund-raising dinner at a Washington Hotel Thursday night and was only minutes from leaving the White House when the tragic news came from Memphis.

The White House said Johnson had telephoned Mrs. King at her home in Atlanta and expressed his sympathy.

The text of President Johnson's statement:

"America is shocked and saddened by the brutal slaying tonight of Dr. Martin Luther King.

"I ask every citizen to reject the blind violence that has struck Dr. King who lived by nonviolence.

"I pray that his family can find comfort in the memory of all he tried to do for the land he loved so well. I have just conveyed the sympathy of Mrs. ...

Associated Press Wirephoto

DR. MARTIN LUTHER KING JR.
Civil Rights Leader Assassinated

Police Nab 2 in Hunt For Killer

MEMPHIS, Tenn. (AP) — Nobel Laureate Martin Luther King Jr., father of non-violence in the American Civil rights movement, was killed by an assassin's bullet Thursday night.

King, 39, was hit in the neck by a bullet as he stood on the balcony of a motel here. He died less than an hour later in St. Joseph Hospital.

Gov. Buford Ellington immediately ordered 4,000 National Guard troops back into the city. A curfew, which was clamped on Memphis after a King-led march turned into a riot a week ago, was reimposed.

Police said incidents of violence, including several fire bombings were reported following King's death.

The 1964 Nobel Peace Prize winner, was standing on the balcony of his motel here, where he had come to lead protests in behalf of the city's 1,300 striking garbage workers, most of them Negroes, when he was shot.

Two unidentified men were arrested several blocks from the motel.

Police also said they found a 30-06 rifle on Main Street about one block from the motel, but it was not confirmed whether this was the weapon that killed King.

An aide who was standing nearby said the shot hit King in the neck and lower right part of his face.

"Martin Luther King is dead," said Asst. Police Chief Henry Lux, the first word of the death.

Asst. Hospital Administrator Paul Hess confirmed later that King died at 7 p.m. of a bullet wound in the neck.

The Rev. Jesse Jackson said he and others in the King party were getting ready to go to dinner when the shooting occurred.

"King was on the second floor balcony of the motel," Jackson said. "He had just bent over. If he had been standing up, he wouldn't have been hit in the face."

King had just told Ben Branch. "My man, be sure to sing 'Blessed Lord' tonight and sing it well."

A shot then rang out, Jackson said.

... the only sound ...

U. S. Leaders Deplore Killing

NEW YORK (AP) — The nation's civil rights and political leaders reacted with anguish, shock and grief Thursday night at the slaying of the Rev. Dr. Martin Luther King Jr. in Memphis.

There also was fear that the slaying could lead to more violence.

"We have been saddened," President Johnson told the nation on radio and television. "I ask every citizen to reject the blind violence that has struck Dr. King who lived in nonviolence."

The President said he was postponing his trip to Hawaii, for a Vietnam strategy conference, until Friday. He had been scheduled to leave about midnight Thursday.

Vice President Hubert H. Humphrey said the slaying "brings shame to our country. An apostle of nonviolence has been the victim of violence."

The vice president said, however, that his death will bring new strength to the cause he fought for.

A spokesman for the National Association for the Advancement of Colored People said, "I am shocked and grieved by this wanton murder of a peace-loving man, a dedicated, courageous man. This murder certainly does not solve anything and it will be deeply resented by Negroes through the country and by other people who believe in nonviolent protest."

State Flags Ordered At Half Staff

NEW YORK (9P)—Gov. Nelson A. Rockefeller ordered flags on all state buildings flown at half-staff Friday "as an expression of the deep sorrow felt by New Yorkers" at the death of Dr. Martin Luther King, Jr.

... statement ... he said Dr. ...

[Joh]nson Defers Trip [Aft]er Murder of Dr. King

[WASHIN]GTON (AP) — Presi[dent Johns]on, preparing for a ... Vietnam strategy ... in Honolulu, delayed [his depar]ture overnight Thurs[day becau]se of the assassination ... his of the Rev. Dr. [Martin L]uther King.

[The P]resident went before ... cameras and radio ...nes to declare Ameri[ca "s]hocked and saddened" [by the t]ragedy. He condemned violence, lawlessness and divisiveness.

Johnson goes to Honolulu amid growing caution here about the prospects of preliminary peace talks.

The White House did not indicate whether Johnson would change his earlier plan to meet at March Air Force Base, Calif., to talk with former President Dwight D. Eisenhower.

The original plan called for Johnson also to meet in Hawaii Sunday with South Korea's president, Chung Hee Park.

Earlier in the day, Hanoi charged that American planes bombed a North Vietnamese town northwest of the country's capital—deep inside the territory the President had declared off limits to U.S. air raiders.

The Pentagon quickly disavowed any "present knowledge of any such U.S. attack since the President's speech, Sunday night" in which he proclaimed the curtailment of U.S. bombing of North Vietnam.

"Nonetheless an immediate investigation has been ordered," Asst. Secretary Phil G. ...

[P]resident Hailed

...

Creating a Holiday

Efforts to make a holiday honoring King began four days after his death. U.S. Congressman John Conyers introduced a bill to create a national holiday. Lawmakers voted against it. Some didn't want a holiday for a private citizen. Others didn't think King deserved a holiday.

Early Celebrations

Coretta Scott King didn't want people to forget her husband. She planned the first event to celebrate his birthday in 1969. Four years later, Illinois made Martin Luther King Jr. Day a holiday. It was the first state to do so. Massachusetts and Connecticut followed in 1974.

Coretta Scott King gives a speech in Washington, D.C., in 1968.

In 1983 more than 500,000 people gathered in Washington, D.C. It was the 20th anniversary of the March on Washington. Six million people had signed ***petitions*** asking Congress to make a holiday for King. The bill passed that year. President Ronald Reagan signed it into law.

petition—a written document that people sign to show that they want a person or organization to do something

President Ronald Reagan signs the paperwork to make Martin Luther King Jr. Day a national holiday.

Celebrations

The first national Martin Luther King Jr. Day was held on January 20, 1986. Atlanta, Georgia, had the biggest celebration. People came to march with the King family. Only 17 states held celebrations the first year. By 2000 all 50 states did.

Local leaders march in San Francisco's first Martin Luther King Jr. Day celebration.

Many schools and government offices are closed on Martin Luther King Jr. Day. Families celebrate by going to parades, picnics, and church services. Some cities have concerts and speeches honoring King.

Fact King was the first private citizen to be honored with a federal holiday.

"50 Years Later: The Journey Continues in Pursuit of the Dream"
THE MARTIN LUTHER KING, JR. MEMORIAL MARCH
Raleigh, North Carolina
January 20, 2014
I AM THE DREAM

King's life was spent serving others. To honor his work, a change was made to his holiday. Congress made it a national day of service in 1994. Now many ***volunteers*** spend the day helping out in their communities.

Fact King once said, "Everybody can be great because anybody can serve."

volunteer—a person who does work without getting paid for it

People can honor King by serving others and fighting for equality. They can help those in need and clean up public places. People can also speak up when others are being treated unfairly. They can continue the work of a man who died trying to make the world better for others.

Onions-Red Baron

Glossary

assassinate (us-SASS-uh-nate)—to murder an important person

civil rights (SI-vil RYTS)—the rights that all people have to be free and treated equally

Congress (KAHNG-gruhs)—the branch of a national government that makes laws

petition (puh-TISH-uhn)—a written document that people sign to show that they want a person or organization to do something

protest (pro-TEST)—an action of a group of people who want something to be changed

segregation (seg-ruh-GAY-shuhn)—the practice of separating people according to groups, especially racial groups

volunteer (vol-uhn-TIHR)—a person who does work without getting paid to do it

Read More

Hooks, Gwendolyn. *If You Were a Kid During the Civil Rights Movement.* If You Were a Kid. New York: Children's Press, an imprint of Scholastic Inc., 2017.

Koestler-Grack, Rachel A. *Martin Luther King, Jr. Day.* Celebrating Holidays. Minneapolis: Bellwether Media, Inc., 2018.

Weakland, Mark. *When Martin Luther King Jr. Wore Roller Skates.* Leaders Doing Headstands. North Mankato, Minn.: Picture Window Books, 2017.

Internet Sites

Use FactHound to find Internet sites related to this book.

Visit www.facthound.com

Just type in 9781977102775 and go.

Critical Thinking Questions

1. Martin Luther King Jr. had a dream. What did he want to see happen?
2. How can you celebrate Martin Luther King Jr. Day?
3. What was one change that came about because of Martin Luther King Jr.'s efforts?

Index

Table of Contents

First Facts are published by Pebble,
1710 Roe Crest Drive, North Mankato, Minnesota 56003
www.mycapstone.com

Library of Congress Cataloging-in-Publication Data
Library of Congress Cataloging-in-Publication data is available on the Library of Congress website.
ISBN 978-1-9771-0279-9 (library binding)
ISBN 978-1-9771-0534-9 (paperback)
ISBN 978-1-9771-0287-4 (eBook PDF)

Editorial Credits
Mandy Robbins, editor; Cynthia Della-Rovere, designer; Pam Mitsakos, media researcher; Tori Abraham, production specialist

Photo Credits
Getty Images: Photographer's Choice/Ariel Skelley, Cover: iStockphoto/M_a_y_a, 16-17; Newscom: akg-images, 10-11, Picture History, 7 (bottom right); North Wind Picture Archives: 7 (top left), 15; Shutterstock: Bokeh Blur, Design Element, Dmytro Balkhovitin, 3, (bottom left), 20-21, Duda Vasillii, Design Element, Everett Historical, 12-13, katjen, 4-5, Roberto Galan, 18-19, sharpner, 1 (bottom); spatuletail, 8-9

Printed and bound in the United States of America.
PA49

Table of Contents

Happy Birthday, America!

Independence Day is the birthday of the United States of America. It celebrates the day the nation declared its independence from Great Britain. Americans celebrate it every year on July 4th.

independence—the state of being free from the control of other people or governments

The Fight for Independence

Before there were states, Americans lived in 13 ***colonies***. They were governed by Great Britain's ***Parliament*** and King George III. When Great Britain needed money, it raised the colonists' ***taxes***. The colonists thought this was unfair. They had no say in Parliament.

colony—an area of land ruled by a faraway country

Parliament—the law-making body of British government

tax—money that people or businesses must give to the government to pay for what the government does

King George III

A colonist named Daniel Dulany wrote this paper speaking out about the new taxes.

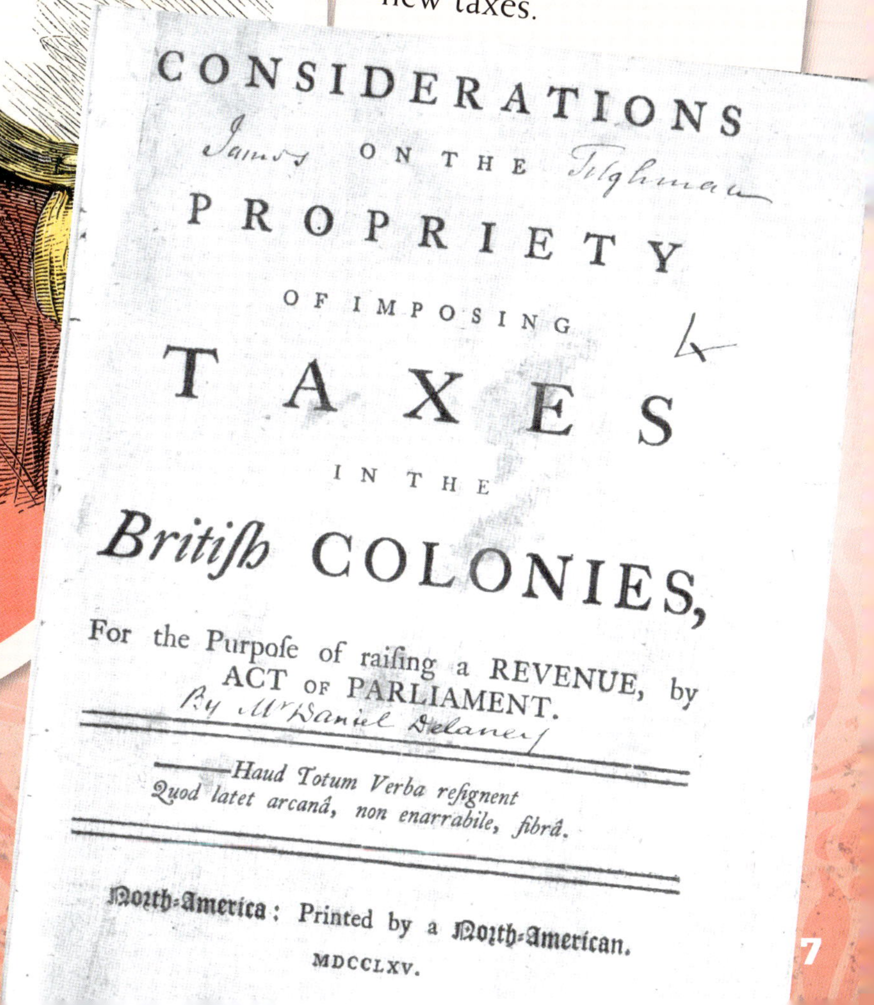

CONSIDERATIONS
ON THE
PROPRIETY
OF IMPOSING
TAXES
IN THE
British COLONIES,
For the Purpose of raising a REVENUE, by ACT OF PARLIAMENT.

Haud Totum Verba resignent
Quod latet arcanâ, non enarrabile, fibrâ.

North-America: Printed by a North-American.
MDCCLXV.

The colonists thought it was unfair that they had no say in British government. They ***protested*** the new laws and taxes. King George III ignored their complaints. He sent soldiers to the colonies to keep order. Many colonists thought it was time to form their own country.

protest—to say you think something is wrong and needs to be changed

During the Boston Tea Party, colonists protested the British tax on tea. They threw crates of British tea into the ocean.

Representatives from all 13 colonies met in 1776. They voted to break away from Great Britain. Thomas Jefferson used their ideas to write the ***Declaration*** of Independence. It was adopted on July 4, 1776.

representative—someone who is chosen to act or speak for others

declaration—an official statement or the document that contains it

Fact John Adams and Benjamin Franklin helped with the Declaration. They made changes before it was voted on.

Colonial leaders sign the Declaration of Independence.

It took more than words to win freedom. The colonists fought the British soldiers in the ***Revolutionary*** War (1775–1783). In the end the colonists won. They no longer lived in colonies. They lived in the United States of America.

Fact George Washington led the ***Continental*** army. He became America's first president.

revolution—an attempt to overthrow a government and replace it with a new system

Continental—relating to the 13 colonies that became the United States

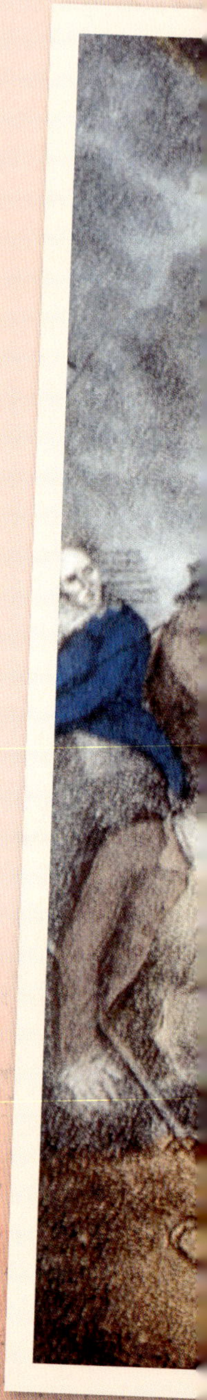

The colonists fight the British during the Battle of Bunker Hill.

Let's Celebrate!

Philadelphia held the first Independence Day celebration on July 4, 1777. The day included speeches, music, and fireworks. Soon other towns began holding celebrations. *Congress* made Independence Day an official holiday in 1870.

Fact Philadelphia was the capital of the United States from 1790 to 1800.

Congress—the branch of a national government that makes laws

Independence Hall in Philadelphia

Independence Day is a giant birthday celebration. Schools, businesses, and government offices shut down. Cities have big parades with bands and floats. Neighborhoods have small parades. Kids decorate their bikes with red, white, and blue streamers. Friends and families have picnics.

Fact All U.S. major-league baseball teams wear red, white, and blue uniforms on Independence Day.

Some songs capture the spirit of Independence Day. Francis Scott Key wrote *The Star-Spangled Banner* in 1814. Today it is the U.S. national ***anthem***. *America the Beautiful* and *God Bless America* are two other ***patriotic*** songs. Marching bands play songs such as these in parades.

anthem—a song of praise, often for one's country

patriotic—feeling or showing love and pride for one's country

John Philip Sousa

John Philip Sousa wrote 136 marches more than 100 years ago. He was known as the "March King." Sousa's *Stars and Stripes Forever* is America's national march.

Across the country, Independence Day ends with a bang. The night sky lights up as bright fireworks burst in the air. The pops and booms sound like the cannons used to win the country's freedom. It is a sparkling reminder of the nation's history.

True Meaning

Independence Day is more than flags, fireworks, and food. It is a day to remember those who created our country. It is also a day to thank members of the military who work to protect it.

Glossary

anthem (AN-thuhm)—a song of praise for one's country

colony (KAH-luh-nee)—land ruled by a faraway country

Congress (KAHNG-gruhs)—the branch of a national government that makes laws

Continental (KAHN-tuh-nen-tuhl)—relating to the 13 colonies that became the United States

declaration (dek-luh-RAY-shuhn)—an official statement or the document that contains it

independence (in-di-PEN-duhnss)—the state of being free from the control of other people or governments

Parliament (PAR-luh-muhnt)—the law-making body of British government

patriotic (pay-tree-OT-ik)—feeling or showing love and pride for one's country

protest (PRO-test)—to say you think something is wrong and needs to be changed

representative (rep-ri-ZEN-tuh-tiv)—someone who is chosen to act or speak for others

revolution (rev-uh-LOO-shun)—an attempt to overthrow a government and replace it with a new system

tax (TAKS)—money that people or businesses must give to the government to pay for what the government does

Read More

Mara, Wil. *If You Were a Kid During the American Revolution.* If You Were a Kid. New York: Children's Press, an imprint of Scholastic Inc., 2017.

Potter, Jonathan. *Why Do We Celebrate Independence Day?* Celebrating U.S. Holidays. New York: PowerKids Press, 2019.

Winter, Jonah. *The Founding Fathers!: Those Horse-Ridin', Fiddle-Playin', Book-Readin', Gun-Totin' Gentlemen Who Started America.* New York: Atheneum Books America, 2015.

Internet Sites

Use FactHound to find Internet sites related to this book.

Visit www.facthound.com

Just type in 9781977102799 and go.

Critical Thinking Questions

1. Why is Independence Day called the birthday of the United States?
2. Why did the 13 colonies want to be free from Great Britain?
3. How do you celebrate Independence Day?

Index